The Tickety Tale Teller

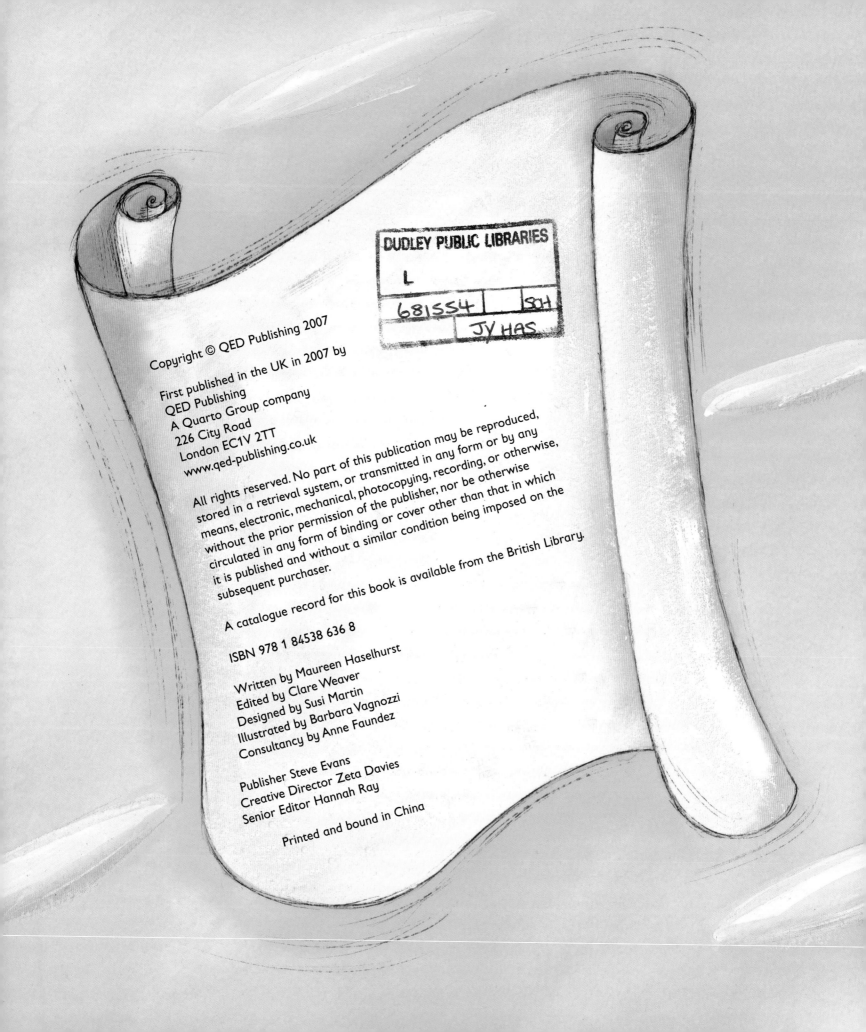

Copyright © QED Publishing 2007

First published in the UK in 2007 by
QED Publishing
A Quarto Group company
226 City Road
London EC1V 2TT
www.qed-publishing.co.uk

A catalogue record for this book is available from the British Library.

ISBN 978 1 84538 636 8

Written by Maureen Haselhurst
Edited by Clare Weaver
Designed by Susi Martin
Illustrated by Barbara Vagnozzi
Consultancy by Anne Faundez

Publisher Steve Evans
Creative Director Zeta Davies
Senior Editor Hannah Ray

Printed and bound in China

The Tickety Tale Teller

Maureen Haselhurst

Illustrated by

Barbara Vagnozzi

QED Publishing

QED

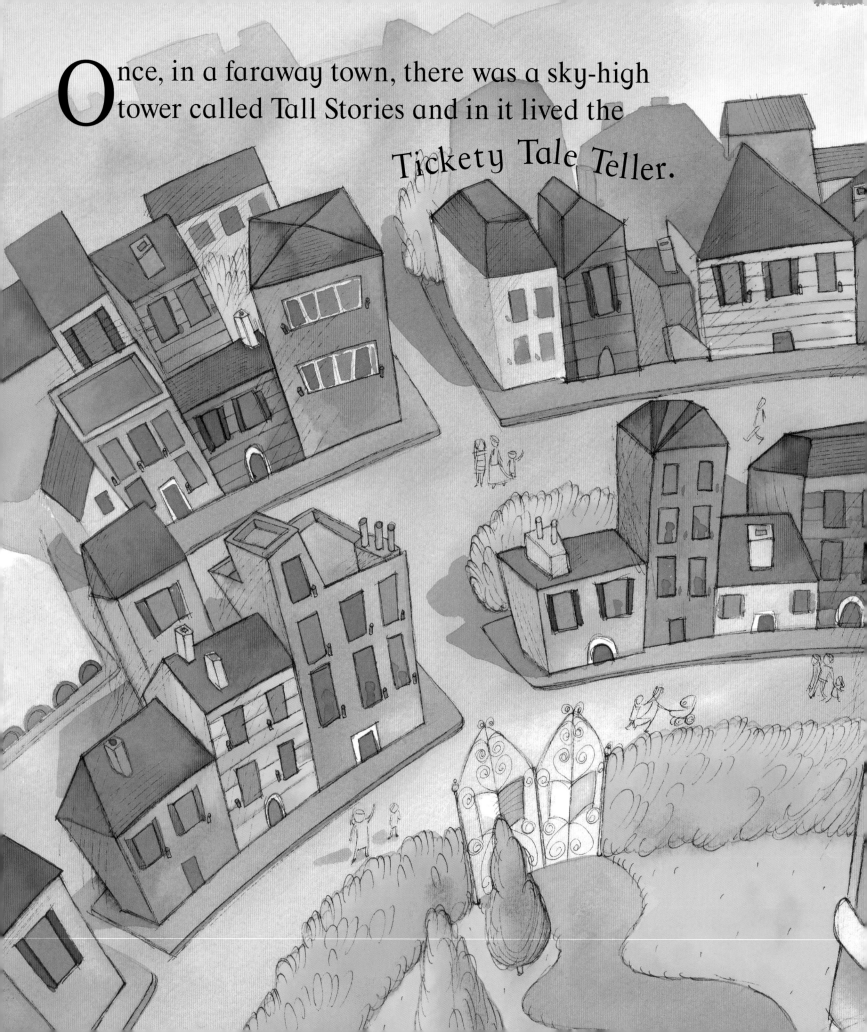

Once, in a faraway town, there was a sky-high tower called Tall Stories and in it lived the Tickety Tale Teller.

Over the long, long years,
she had filled the rooms
with her wonderful tales,
until Tall Stories was
bursting with books.

Whenever the children in the town below wanted to hear a story, they would fly a flag from their window.

A dragon flag for a fairy story,
a star flag for a space story,
a ship for a pirate story and so on.

Every day, the Tickety Tale Teller would look down at the flags from her sky-scraping tower and say to herself,

"Another story, quickety-quick!
I'll be there in a tickety-tick",

and grabbing a bundle of books, she would slide, helter-skelter down her banister and scoot out of the door.

She became busier and busier. Everyone wanted a story. Bedtimes were a hurly-burly of comings and goings as she scurried from house to house.

The poor Tickety Tale Teller
was rushed off her feet!

It would be so much easier if she could
tell all the children a story at the same
time – but how? And then she had an idea!

That evening, a huge hot-air balloon appeared over the town. It floated lower and lower, bumping into the buildings as it went. People flung open their windows just in time to hear a voice bellow,

"Once upon a time..."

Inside the balloon's basket was the Tickety Tale Teller holding a giant megaphone.

"Please go away!"
shouted the children.
"You're waking us up!
Besides, we want to be
read a story properly."

She went away.

Ah well, she
already had
another idea.

The following evening,
great glittering fountains of sparks
glowed in the sky above the town.

Fireworks!

People flung open their windows
as a bright finger of fire wrote,

"Once upon a time..."

and then fizzled out as the
air whooshed and whizzed
and whirly-gigged.

"Please go away!"

shouted the children. "You're waking
us up! Besides, we want to be
told a story properly."

For many days, no one saw
the Tickety Tale Teller. The
children flew their story flags
but she never came.

Do not
disturb

Inside Tall Stories there
was a flurry of housework
as, room by room, the
Tickety Tale Teller cleared
the shelves of books.

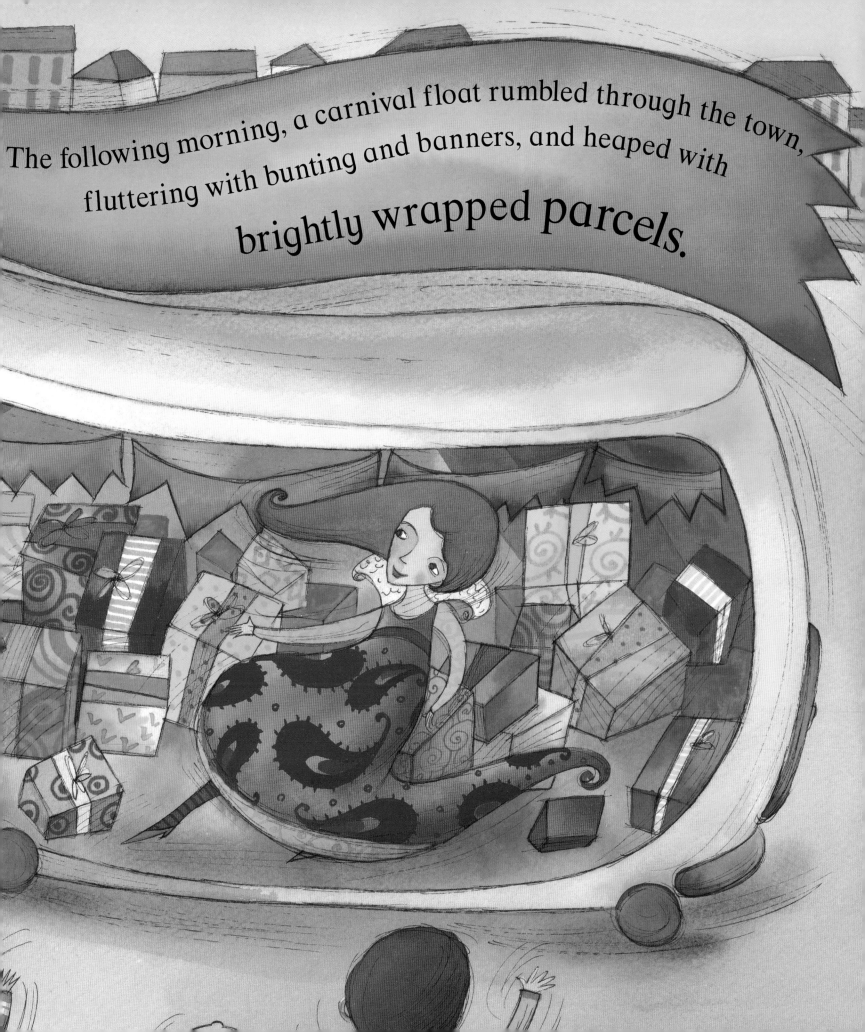

The following morning, a carnival float rumbled through the town, fluttering with bunting and banners, and heaped with brightly wrapped parcels.

Out jumped the Tickety Tale Teller and she scooted from door to door, popping a parcel through every letterbox.

Inside each parcel
was a storybook with
a note saying,

Please read this tale
to the children
— until they can
read it to you.

And so it was that everyone in the town became a story-teller. It was now their turn to fill Tall Stories with tales of their own.

As for the Tickety Tale Teller, it was
time to move on to another town.

Climbing into her balloon she floated away,

scattering a trail of brightly
wrapped tales.

Notes for Teachers and Parents

- Using shoe boxes, build a model Tall Stories tower. Fill the rooms with books of different genres. Ask the children to write a story of their own to be stored in a special room at the top of the tower. Using blocks etc., build a town at the foot of the tower and choose a name for it. Encourage the children to imagine what might happen in their town. Who lives there? Who built it? What goes on there?

- Design flags with pictures to tell the Tickety Tale Teller what kind of tales the children would like to hear. Display the flags like bunting on a washing-line.

- If the children have access to a chute or slide, they can play at being the Tickety Tale Teller sliding down her banister and chanting, "Another story, quickety-quick! I'll be there in a tickety-tick."

- Make a model hot-air balloon using a helium-filled balloon. The basket can be made with a painted egg carton suspended by ribbons, wool or string and decorated, for example, with metal foil, ribbons and feathers. Hang it from the ceiling or a window recess.

- Create a collage of a firework display using coloured foil, glitter and sequins against a dark background. Ask the children to think of words to describe what they would see, hear and smell and how they would feel, and include the words on the collage. In music lessons, compose firework music with drums, tambourines, triangles, whistles, kazoos and other instruments.

- Sort out the bookshelves and ask each child to choose a favourite book, the title of which they must keep secret. They then gift-wrap their choice. Each piece of gift wrap is labelled in advance with the name of another child. When the parcels are opened, the children read their book (or have it read to them) and then guess who might have chosen that book.

- Play the Tickety Tale memory game. Place items from the story onto a covered tray – for example, book, sparkler, gift wrap, flag, balloon. The children look at the items for one minute and then the tray is covered again. How many items can they remember?

- Make a Tickety Snakes and Ladders game using banisters as snakes and the stairs in the house as ladders. Tiny gift-wrapped parcels, such as those used in table confetti, could be used as counters.

- Set up a story chain – one child begins to tell a story, which is then taken up by the others, until it reaches its conclusion. Some children will be more comfortable retelling a familiar story, while others will be confident enough to create their own.

- Have a pass-the-parcel story-reading session, using a bag containing several books. When the music stops, the children chant, "With a tickety-tick, choose a story, quickety-quick! Close your eyes and take your pick." The child holding the bag chooses a story, which is read aloud either by the adult or by the child, and the process is repeated.